I am unselfish when I

_____

TROPICAL BIRDWING/PHOTOGRAPH BY DR. E. R. DEGGINGER

_____   _____
name   date

Solomon John
and the
Terrific Truck

A BOOK ABOUT UNSELFISHNESS

Kersten Hamilton
Illustrated by Raoul Soto

Chariot Books™
David C. Cook Publishing Co.

Chariot Books™ is an imprint of David C. Cook Publishing Co.
David C. Cook Publishing Co., Elgin, Illinois 60120
David C. Cook Publishing Co., Weston, Ontario
SOLOMON JOHN AND THE TERRIFIC TRUCK
© 1990 David C. Cook Publishing Co., Elgin, IL
All rights reserved.
First Printing, 1990. Printed in the United States of America
94 93 92 91 90 5 4 3 2 1
ISBN 1-55513-978-7 LC 89-60099

The verse marked (TLB) is taken from *The Living Bible* ©1971, owned by assignment by Illinois Regional Bank N.A. (as trustee). Used by permission of Tyndale House Publishers Inc., Wheaton, IL 60189. All rights reserved.

Solomon John was the littlest one.

His oldest brother drove a car and climbed mountains with a rope.

"Dave the Brave," said Solomon John.

"How's my man?" said Dave.

Solomon John's next oldest brother rode a
skateboard and had a secret club that met in a tree.
"Bart the Brat," said Solomon John.
"Babies can't join the club," said Bart.

One day the mailman brought a box from Grandma.

There was a leather baseball mitt for Dave.

There was a Zippy-Speedo-Whammer-Riffic truck for Bart.

There was a jack-in-the-box for Solomon John.
"That's a baby toy," said Bart.

"Can I look at your truck?" asked Solomon
John.

"No. It's MINE. Go play with your baby toys,"
said Bart.

Solomon John's fingers itched. They wanted to
touch the Zippy-Speedo-Whammer-Riffic truck.

Bart pushed the truck down the hall to his room. He left it sitting on the floor.

Solomon John crept into the room. He touched the Zippy-Speedo-Whammer-Riffic truck with one finger.

"What are you doing in MY room?" yelled Bart.

Solomon John went to his room. He crawled under the bed to his secret place. Jesus was the only one who could find him there.

"Jesus," he said, "Why don't You teach that Bart to share?"

Then he heard the ice-cream man coming down the street. He had two quarters in his pocket. A Fudgsicle would make him feel better.

The ice-cream man stopped at the curb.
"I would like a double Fudgsicle, please," said
Solomon John.

"Hey, buddy," said Bart. "Can I have some of your Fudgsicle?"

Solomon John felt like saying, "It's MINE." He
licked a chocolate drip off his finger.
"PULLEEZZZ?" said Bart.

Solomon John thought about Jesus. Jesus said to
eat others the way you want them to treat you. He
ondered if Jesus meant even Bart the Brat.

"Okay," he said. He broke the Fudgsicle in two.

"Hey, you're not such a bad kid," said Bart.
"Want to play with my Zippy-Speedo-Whammer-Riffic truck?"

"Sure," said Solomon John.

"I get the first turn," said Bart.